Trolls Go Home!

Trolls Go Home!

by Alan MacDonald

illustrations by Mark Beech

BLOOMSBURY

PRIDDLES: Roger, Jackie and Warren
Description: 'Pasty-faced peeples'
Likes: Peace and quiet
Dislikes: Trolls

MR TROLL: Egbert / Eggy
Description : Tall, dark
and scaresome
Likes: Roaring, tromping,
hiding under bridges

MRS TROLL: Nora
Description: Gorgeous
(ask Mr Troll)
Likes: Huggles and kisses,
caves, the dark

ULRIK TROLL
Description: Big for his age
Likes: Smells, singing,
Rockball

GOAT
Description:
Strong-smelling,
beardy beast
Likes: Mountains, grass
Dislikes: Being eaten

To Sally with trollish love – A.M.

To Robyn and Duncan for their ongoing
support and encouragement – M.B.

First published in Great Britain in 2006 by Bloomsbury Publishing plc
36 Soho Square, London, WID 3QY

A CIP catalogue record of this book is available from the British Library

ISBN 978 0 7475 8473 5

All papers used by Bloomsbury Publishing are natural, recyclable
products made from wood grown in well-managed forests.
The manufacturing processes conform to the environmental
regulations of the country of origin.

Printed in Great Britain by Clays Ltd, St Ives Plc

1 3 5 7 9 10 8 6 4 2

www.bloomsbury.com

Tall, Dark and Ugly

'JACKIE! Come and see! They're moving in next door!'

Mr Priddle had his telescope trained on a large blue removal van standing in next door's drive. His wife's voice floated up the stairs.

'Roger! I hope you're not snooping through that telescope?'

'Of course I'm not,' said Mr Priddle, with his eye pressed to the lens. 'Wait! They're getting out! I can see . . . Good gravy!'

'What, dear?' Mrs Priddle came into the front

bedroom holding two mugs of tea. She was followed by her freckle-faced son Warren, who had come upstairs to find out what all the fuss was about.

'They're huge! Colossal!' exclaimed Mr Priddle.

'Well, some people *are* tall,' replied his wife. 'Just because you're a bit on the short side, Roger.'

'No, I mean *really* huge, Jackie. Take a look for yourself.'

Mrs Priddle folded her arms. 'I am not snooping on the neighbours through a telescope. What will they think if they see you peering through the curtains?'

'I don't mind snooping,' offered Warren. 'Let me have a look!'

'In a minute, Warren,' said Mr Priddle impatiently. 'Good Lord! I've never seen anyone so hairy!'

'Well, what if they are?' replied Mrs Priddle. 'Just because you're bald as a newborn baby.'

'I don't just mean *hairy*. I mean hairy *all over*,' said Mr Priddle.

'Now you're being ridiculous!'

'See for yourself!' said Mr Priddle.

'Let me look! It's my turn!' cried Warren, making a grab for the telescope.

'Get your hands off, Warren!' snapped his dad.

'Don't be so childish, Roger,' said Mrs Priddle. 'Let the boy have a go.'

Warren pushed in front of his dad. Covering one eye, he used the other to squint through the lens. He could see one of the neighbours carrying a table towards the front door. The table was like the base of a tree trunk, but the creature – he couldn't really call it a person – carried it as if it was no heavier than a matchstick.

'Woah! *Ugly* or what?' said Warren.

'Warren!' scolded his mother. 'It's not nice to say that about people.'

'But Mum, they *are* ugly,' Warren pointed out.

'He's right, Jackie,' agreed Mr Priddle. 'They're brutes. From what I've seen they belong in a zoo, not a house.' He elbowed his son aside so that he could reapply himself to the telescope.

'You're making it all up,' said Mrs Priddle.

'We're not! Take a look for yourself!'

'I told you I am not spying on our neighbours

through a telescope. It's rude.' Mrs Priddle took a dainty sip of her tea.

'There's another one getting out,' pointed Warren excitedly. 'There are three of them!'

'Move over,' said Mrs Priddle. She smoothed back her blonde curls and put her eye to the telescope.

'Oh, my giddy bananas!' she said. 'I don't feel well.'

The Trolls moving into Number 10 would have been a surprising sight for anyone. Mr Troll was wearing a white vest, a baseball cap and an enormous pair of bright red Bermuda shorts reaching to his knees. These were the only clothes he could find in the shop that were big enough to fit him. Mrs Troll was wearing a flowery cotton dress jammed so tightly over her body that at any moment the buttons threatened to burst off and shoot in all directions. Only their young son Ulrik looked halfway normal. But it was difficult for any troll to look normal standing in Mountain View, Biddlesden this sunny morning.

The Trolls had coarse brown hair sprouting all over their bodies. It hid their faces apart from their coal-black eyes, their snoutish noses and the two sharp white fangs that stuck up either side of their mouths. Most trolls cannot be called beautiful. In fact, if you came upon a troll unexpectedly – say by wandering into a deep, dark forest – you would probably scream and climb the nearest tree quicker than a startled squirrel. A troll's sheer size is enough to scare anyone. Their ugliness is legendary, enough to put a witch or a hag off their breakfast. Mr Troll was roughly the size of a grizzly bear standing on its hind legs – and next to him Roger Priddle would have looked like a stick insect on a diet. Even their new house at Number 10 looked rather small, as Mr Troll found out when he tried to get the table through the front door.

'Arghh! Gnnnh!' he roared. 'It's too small.'

'It can't be too small,' said Mrs Troll, 'it's the same size as it always was.'

'Not the table,' groaned Mr Troll. 'The door! The door's too small for me to get in!'

'Well, use your head then,' sighed Mrs Troll.

Mr Troll did. He thumped his big hairy head against the door frame and the plaster above it caved in, leaving a space large enough for him to squeeze through with the table.

Next door, Mr Priddle gasped. 'Did you see that? He smashed the door to pieces! With his head!'

'I hope he's not going to do that every time he comes home,' said Mrs Priddle.

Inside Number 10, the Trolls looked around their new home. Sunny yellow wallpaper brightened the walls and there were carpets on the floor.

Mr Troll sniffed. 'It's very clean,' he grumbled.

'Don't worry, Egbert,' said Mrs Troll, 'we'll soon change that. A nice bit of dirt on the floor, a few mouldy leaves – it'll soon look like home.'

'I like it as it is,' said Ulrik. 'Much better than our old cave.'

Mr and Mrs Troll exchanged dark looks. Ulrik ran into the hall.

'Uggsome! There are stairs! Can I look up here, Mum?' he called, jumping up them two at a time.

In the bathroom, the Trolls stared at the gleaming white bath.

'What is it, Mum?' asked Ulrik.

'It's a bath, my hairling,' explained Mrs Troll. 'You lie down in it.'

Ulrik climbed in and lay down. It was a tight fit,

even for a young troll. His large hairy feet stuck
out beyond the end of the bath. 'What's this?' he
asked, twisting a silver tap round. The shower
came on above, soaking him with a hundred tiny
jets of water. 'Ha ha! It's tickly!' Ulrik giggled.
'I'm all wet!'

'Get out of there, Ulrik,' growled Mr Troll. 'The
rain's coming in.'

'It's not rain, it's a shower,' explained Mrs Troll,
turning off the tap. 'I read that peeples take a

shower every day. To keep themselves clean.'

'Clean?' said Mr Troll, recoiling in horror. 'You mean they wash? With water?'

'Yes, and something called soap.'

'I want to wash with a soap!' shouted Ulrik.

Mr and Mrs Troll exchanged another worried glance.

'We don't want you smelling all sweet as a daisy,' growled Mr Troll. 'Trolls smell of the forest, the earth, the dark. Those are the old Trollish smells.'

Ulrik sniffed himself under his hairy arms. He liked his own smell. He wondered what peeples smelled like up close. Next time he got the chance he would make sure to smell one.

By supper time they were all hungry. It had been a long journey coming from the far blue mountains of Norway. Mrs Troll set a single tin on the table in front of them. Mr Troll pointed at it with his fork. 'What's this?'

'It's called Baked Bean,' said Mrs Troll. 'I got it at the shop on the corner.'

Mr Troll screwed up his nose in disgust. 'Bean? I can't eat bean – what kind of a meal is that? Trolls eat meat! Where's the goat pie?'

Mrs Troll sighed. 'We're not at home now, Egbert. I don't think it's as easy to find goat.'

'No goat pie?' Mr Troll's mouth fell open.

'Don't blame me,' said Mrs Troll. 'It was you that wanted to move here.'

'We didn't have any choice, you know very well,' said Mr Troll darkly. 'How could we stay after what happened?'

'What did happen?' asked Ulrik innocently. His parents had never explained why they'd left home in such a hurry. Mr Troll covered his face with his hands.

'I don't want to talk about it.'

'He'll have to know sometime,' said Mrs Troll.

'Know what?' demanded Ulrik.

'Ulrik,' said Mrs Troll, 'your dad had a nasty experience. With a goat.'

'No! Don't speak about it!' groaned Mr Troll.

'He's got a right to know,' insisted Mrs Troll. 'Are you going to tell him or shall I?'

Mr Troll peered at his son over his hands. 'It was a monster, Ulrik,' he said. 'A monster!'

'It was a billy goat, Egbert,' said Mrs Troll. 'Don't exaggerate.'

Mr Troll looked at his son. 'A giant goat, Ulrik. He had two brothers but next to him they were only tiddlers. I faced him on the bridge. He had hooves like iron, hornses as sharp as knives.'

'What happened, Dad?' asked Ulrik, wide-eyed. 'Did you roar and chase him away?'

Mr Troll shook his head, unable to speak the awful truth.

Mrs Troll took over. 'The goat charged,' she said. 'Your father lost his nerve and he got tossed from the bridge into the river. I had to drag him out by the ears, or he would have drowned.'

'The shame of it,' moaned Mr Troll. 'The shame!'

'So you see, Ulrik, that's why we had to move,' continued Mrs Troll. 'Your father felt that if we stayed at home the other trolls would always be making fun of him.'

'Beated by a goat! How could I look them in the eye again?' asked Mr Troll pitifully.

Ulrik went over to his dad and stroked his large, shaggy head. 'Never mind, Dad. I bet those other trolls would have run away.'

'You think so?' Mr Troll managed a smile.

'You faced a giant goat,' said Ulrik. 'I think you're the bravest dad in the whole world.'

Mr Troll gave his son a squeeze. He wiped away a speck of dirt that was making his eyes water. 'What about this bean then, Ulrik? I'm starving,' he said.

Opening the tin was harder than Mrs Troll had expected. She watched Ulrik trying to bite into it with his sharp teeth, but even a troll's teeth couldn't make much of an impression. Mrs Troll tried cutting the can with a knife and fork, but each time it catapulted across the table like a slippery fish.

All this time, Mr Troll's face was growing darker and darker. He was starting to growl – a sure sign that he was about to lose his temper. (Trolls have short tempers at the best of times and Mr Troll liked to boast he had the shortest temper of anyone he knew.) Finally he reached out and grabbed the tin and flung it against the far wall with a great angry roar.

'GRARRR!'

The tin burst open and a thick gloop of baked beans in tomato sauce began to slide down the wallpaper. Ulrik reached out a finger and dipped it in the sauce, licking it off with his tongue.

'Yum!' he said. 'Baked bean is uggsome!'

But Mr Troll had stormed out of the house, banging the door behind him.

Outside the sight of the neat green lawn and the sickly-sweet smell of the roses did nothing to improve his mood. All he could see for miles around were rows of identical houses. They had lawns and patios, wooden benches and flowers in neat borders.

Biddlesden wasn't a bit like home.

He missed the lofty mountains of Norway with

their heads in the clouds. He missed the wide open skies, the shadowy pine forests and the deep lakes that shone like mirrors.

The stars were coming out in the night sky. He looked for the North Star, turned his face in the direction of home and sighed deeply.

A small, warm hand crept into his own and, looking down, he saw little Ulrik at his side.

'Never mind, Dad,' said Ulrik. 'Maybe we'll have goat pie for supper tomorrow.'

'Humph!' said Mr Troll. 'Let's go in. You can lick that bean juice off the wall.'

As they went up the path, Ulrik thought he saw a curtain twitch in an upstairs room next door.

Roaring Lessons

ROGER Priddle liked Sunday mornings. What he liked best was lazing in bed, knowing he didn't have to go to work at the bank. But on this Sunday morning his doze was disturbed by a deafening noise. It sounded as if a herd of wildebeest were stampeding through the house next door. Was it his imagination or was the room shaking? He looked up at the lamp hanging from the ceiling – it was definitely swaying to and fro.

He prodded his wife in the back. 'Wake up, Jackie! I think it's an earthquake!'

'Uh? What?' said Mrs Priddle.

'An earthquake! We're all going to die!'

'Don't be daft, Roger,' his wife yawned sleepily. 'This is Biddlesden we don't have earthquakes. Not on Sundays.'

Then came the bellow from next door that made them both sit upright and clutch at the duvet.

'What was that?' said Mrs Priddle. 'It sounded like someone being murdered!'

'It's that lot next door,' said Mr Priddle grimly.

'Do something, Roger,' urged his wife. 'It's seven o' clock in the morning. Go round and tell them to stop.'

'Are you mad?' asked Mr Priddle. 'Have you seen the size of them?'

'Well, we can't just lie here and listen to that racket.'

The thumps and roars from next door were growing louder. Mrs Priddle banged on the wall with her slipper. No one seemed to hear her.

At Number 10, Ulrik had woken up early. It was impossible to sleep when you were living in a new house where there were so many things to see.

He ran into his parents' room, where he found them both asleep. Under their considerable weight the bed sagged in the middle like a hammock. Ulrik jumped on top of his dad's round belly, rising and falling in time with his snores, until Mr Troll woke up.

'Come on, Dad!' said Ulrik. 'Time for my roaring practice.'

Mr Troll groaned. 'Isn't it a bit early?'

'You said I had to practise every day.'

'All right, all right.'

A few minutes later they were marching round the bedroom, stamping their feet as if they were crushing invisible ants. Sitting up in bed, Mrs Troll watched her son proudly as he followed behind his dad, copying him.

'Remember,' said Mr Troll, 'trolls don't walk. They tromp. They make the trees shake and the birdses twitter away.'

'I like birdses, Dad.'

'Are you tromping?'

'Yes Dad,' said Ulrik.

'Now imagine there is a goat just around the corner and you're going to scare it.'

'Why do I want to scare it?'

'Because you're a troll. Trolls jump out and scare goatses. That's what we do.'

'Couldn't I just say: "Hello, I'm Ulrik"?'

'That's not going to scare anything.'

'Or I could sing them a song. Mum says she likes my singing.'

Mr Troll rolled his eyes.

'Look, is this singing practice or roaring practice?'

'Roaring practice,' admitted Ulrik.

'Then let's get on with it. Roar after me.'

Mr Troll gathered himself. He took a deep breath, swelled out his hairy chest, threw back his head and let rip a roar like a thunderclap.

'GRAAARRR!'

This was the sound that made the Priddles sit bolt upright in bed, fearing that someone was being murdered.

'Now you try,' said Mr Troll.

Ulrik gathered himself. He took a deep breath and tried to swell out his chest like his dad.

Catching sight of himself in the mirror, with his eyes screwed up and his cheeks puffed out, he thought he looked like a wrinkled old goblin. He fell back on the bed, giggling. Mr Troll patted his young son on the head.

'Never mind. We'll have another practice tomorrow,' he said.

As Ulrik ran off to play, Mr Troll shook his head in despair.

'See what I mean? Harmless as a kitten.'

'He's only young, hairling. Give him time,' said Mrs Troll. 'I'm sure they'll have roaring lessons at school.'

Later that morning, Mr Priddle trained his telescope on next door's back garden. He had moved it into Warren's bedroom, where he had a better view from the window.

'What are they doing now, Dad?' asked Warren.

'Shhh!' said Mr Priddle. 'He's just come out. The big one.'

'He's a troll,' said Warren unexpectedly.

'A what? How do you know?' asked his dad.

'I looked it up last night,' said Warren proudly. 'It's in my junior encyclopedia.'

He showed his dad a picture of two large, snarling trolls – a male and female standing side by side. They weren't wearing Bermuda shorts or flowery summer dresses, but the resemblance was unmistakable. He read the caption below the picture.

'*Trolls: fierce race of creatures found in the mountains of Norway. They inhabit caves and underground dwellings.*'

'Good gravy!' said Mr Priddle.

'But what are they doing here, Dad?' asked Warren.

Mr Priddle shrugged. 'I don't know. But he certainly looks mean. A brute. I wouldn't want to tackle him. With my judo skills I might get carried away and do him some serious damage.'

Mr Priddle had once taken up judo at an evening class. It seemed to involve wearing baggy white pyjamas and talking a lot about belts. Actually, he had only attended one of the classes and had returned home grumbling that he'd been chucked around all night like a beach ball. Still, he liked to give the impression that he knew a thing or two about self-defence.

Mrs Priddle came in and joined them by the window. Next door they could see Mr Troll prowling around the garden. He appeared to be marking out a large area in the flower bed.

'What's he up to now? He's down on his hands and knees,' said Mr Priddle.

'Perhaps he's weeding,' said Mrs Priddle.

'No. He's . . . Good heavens! He's digging with his bare hands. Digging up the flowers!' said Mr Priddle.

Showers of earth flew into the air behind Mr Troll as he tore up the flower bed in much the same way as a dog digs up a bone.

'What's he digging for, Dad?' asked Warren.

'How should I know?' said Mr Priddle. 'Perhaps he wants to bury something.'

'You mean like gold – or diamonds?' said his wife hopefully.

'Or a dead body,' said Warren, in a low voice. They both looked at their son nervously and then back at the troll next door.

'It's certainly going to be a big hole,' said Mr Priddle. 'He's going down deep.'

'Maybe he's a murderer,' said Warren. 'Maybe they murder people and bury them in the garden.'

Mrs Priddle let out a faint scream. 'They're living next door! It's not right, Roger. Why didn't they move in next to the Snorleys along the road? Why us? How do you expect me to sleep at night?'

'Now steady, Jackie,' said Mr Priddle.

'I can't be steady. My nerves won't stand it, Roger. I want you to get rid of them.'

Mr Priddle put his arm around his wife. 'Don't you worry, sugarplum,' he said. 'I have a plan.'

'Are you going to fight him, Dad?' asked Warren hopefully. 'Are you going to get him in a head-lock?'

'No,' said Mr Priddle, drawing a red notebook from his pocket. 'I'm going to keep a diary.'

Teachers Are Funny

ULRIK stood in the garden looking at the hole his dad had dug in the flower bed. Where rosebushes had once bloomed, now there was only a tall mound of earth. Ulrik scrambled to the top and looked round. He caught sight of two eyes peering over the garden wall at him. They belonged to one of the neighbours – a plump, freckled boy with rosy cheeks. Ulrik waved to him and the two eyes promptly vanished from sight. He went over to the wall and found the boy crouched beneath it.

'Who are you hiding from?' he whispered.

Warren Priddle sprang to his feet in alarm and backed away. 'Nothing . . . I . . . I think my mum's calling me,' he stammered, making for the back door.

'Don't go,' said Ulrik. 'What's your name?'

'Warren,' said Warren.

'I'm Ulrik.'

'You're a troll,' observed Warren. He was taking care not to get too close.

'Yes,' nodded Ulrik. 'And you're a peeples. Do you go to school?'

'Of course. Everyone goes to school,' said Warren scornfully. He decided the creature wasn't going to eat him after all.

'I'm starting school tomorrow,' said Ulrik proudly. 'It's my first day. We could go together!'

Warren tried to imagine walking into the school playground with Ulrik. His friends would soon start avoiding him if he hung around with this hairy, ugly creature. He didn't want Ulrik telling everyone at school they were friends. For that matter he wasn't sure he wanted a troll at his school at all. He would have to find a way to get rid of him.

'So. You've never been to school then?' he said.

'Never,' said Ulrik. 'Trolls don't have schools, but my dad's been teaching me. So far I've done roaring and tromping. 'Want to see?'

Ulrik tromped up and down the garden, stamping his feet and giving his best roar.

'Great,' said Warren, when he'd finished.

'Is it?' said Ulrik. 'My dad says my roar wouldn't scare a caterpillar.'

'You should do that at school – all that roaring stuff,' said Warren. 'Mrs Melly will love it.'

'Who's Mrs Melly?'

'Our teacher. We call her Mrs Smelly.'

'Mrs Smelly,' repeated Ulrik. He was a little confused. Perhaps teachers had two names.

'I suppose you've never met a teacher either?' said Warren.

'Never,' admitted Ulrik.

'Better be careful,' Warren advised him. 'Teachers can be funny.'

'Can they?'

'Yes. For instance, when you meet Mrs Melly, she'll probably do this.' He held out his hand to Ulrik. Ulrik looked at it, baffled.

'Why?'

'It's polite. That's how we say hello.'

'Oh, I see!' said Ulrik. 'And what do I do?'

Warren gave a weasel smile. 'You bite it.'

'Are you sure?' said Ulrik doubtfully.

'Of course. Give it a good, hard bite or she'll think you're rude.'

Ulrik shrugged. 'OK. Like this?' He took hold of Warren's pink hand and sunk his fangs into it.

'Arrrgh!' yelled Warren. 'Let go!'

'Was that hard enough?' asked Ulrik.

Warren nursed his hand. His eyes were watering. 'Perfect,' he winced. 'Do it like that and Mrs Smelly will love it. She'll probably give you a gold star.'

'Uggsome!' said Ulrik. 'I've never had a gold star!'

Ulrik watched Warren go back inside the house. His hand seemed to be bothering him. Ulrik was glad that he'd made a new friend. Not all peeples he'd met were friendly – some of them ran away just when you wanted to talk to them. But Warren seemed to like him and it was kind of him to explain about teachers' funny ideas. Ulrik couldn't wait to start school tomorrow. Wouldn't his parents be proud when he came home wearing a gold star?

A Nice Kid

THAT afternoon Mrs Troll took Ulrik to the supermarket. She had tried asking for goat again in the local shop, but they only seemed to have tins of the baked bean and something called spagotty hoops. She was pretty sure Mr Troll wouldn't like it any better than the bean. He had been sulking a lot since they'd arrived in Biddlesden and Mrs Troll felt he needed some nice goat pie to cheer him up. She was sure the supermarket would sell goat, perhaps even a young kid, which was Egbert's favourite.

Ulrik had never been in a supermarket. In fact this was only the second time he'd been in a shop, so everything seemed new and exciting. It took some time before Mrs Troll could drag him away from running in and out of the automatic doors. She let him push the trolley with the squeaky wheels and he scooted up and down, dodging in and out of startled shoppers who leapt out of his way.

'What are those, Mum? Can we try them? Please, Mum!' he begged. He was so excited that he forgot to look where he was going and crashed into the back of a young man in a blue jacket.

'Careful!' said the shop assistant, turning to glare at him.

'Sorry,' said Ulrik. He pointed at the trolley. 'I said "Stop!" but it didn't listen.'

Mrs Troll came puffing up the aisle, out of breath.

'Ulrik! I told you not to go charging off on your own!'

'Sorry, Mum, but look! I found where they keep the meatses.'

Ulrik pointed at the shelves either side of the aisle, stacked with meat of every kind.

Mrs Troll addressed the shop assistant politely. 'I was wondering, where do you keep the goat?'

'The what, madam?'

'The goat. Egbert likes goat pie, you see – it's his favourite – but so far I haven't been able to find it.'

'We have turkey,' said the assistant. He pointed to the rows and rows of meat. 'Chicken, lamb, beef, pork . . .'

'No, it has to be goat.'

The assistant scratched his head. No one had ever asked him for goat before.

'What about a kid?' suggested Mrs Troll.

'A kid?' said the assistant.

'Yes, a nice young kid. Tender, not too stringy. Egbert would love that.'

A blonde-haired woman, who was passing with her trolley at that moment, stifled a scream.

'I could roast it over a fire,' said Mrs Troll.

'Yum!' said Ulrik. 'Roast kid!'

'I'm sorry,' said the assistant. 'We don't . . .'

But he didn't get any further. The blonde-haired woman had fainted, passing out face down in her shopping trolley so that it overbalanced with a terrific crash.

'Roger, you won't believe it!' said Mrs Priddle as soon as she burst through the kitchen door. 'I heard the most terrible thing at the supermarket.'

'I'm just making some tea,' said Mr Priddle.

'I don't want tea. I want you to call the police. It's just as I thought – we're living next door to murderers. And worse than that . . .' She lowered her voice and shut the kitchen door. 'They're *cannibals*,' she hissed.

'Cannibals? Who? What are you talking about?' said Roger.

'I told you. I was in the supermarket, minding my own business, and there she was.'

'Who, Jackie? Slow down!'

'Her – from next door! Who do you think?'

'Mrs Troll, you mean?'

She looked at him in surprise. 'How do you know her name?'

'Warren told me. It seems he's been chatting to the young one in the garden.'

'Chatting? You let him *speak* to one of them? Are you out of your mind?'

'Don't worry, darling, he's fine. Just tell me what happened.'

'Well, she – Mrs Troll or whatever she calls herself – was talking to one of the shop assistants. And I heard her bold as you like. "I want a nice young *kid*," she said. "A kid to roast for dinner!"'

'A kid? What do you mean?'

'I mean a *kid*, Roger! A kid! Like our little Warren!'

'Good Lord! You can't be serious!'

'I heard her with my own ears. They cook them over a fire, Roger!'

Mr Priddle gasped and sat down heavily on a chair. It was a nightmare. Their next-door neighbours were cannibals! Monsters! Child-eaters! That would explain why the young one was so keen to 'make friends' with Warren. He was lining up his next meal. Suddenly Mr Priddle remembered something else.

'Jackie! He's going to Warren's school,' he said.

'Who?'

'Ulrik. The young one. Warren says he starts school tomorrow.'

Jackie let out a dramatic scream. She thought about fainting a second time, but her husband was the only one in the room and he wasn't much of an audience.

'We've got to do something,' she said. 'I'm calling the police.' She picked up the phone but before she could dial, Mr Priddle took the receiver from her and replaced it.

'Let's think about this, Jackie,' he said. 'If you tell the police now, they'll never believe you. Think how it will sound – cannibals living in Mountain View. They'll think you've lost your marbles. No, first we've got to gather evidence.'

'How? I'm not sitting here waiting for them to eat somebody,' said Mrs Priddle. 'They've probably had the paper boy already. What about my poor little Warren – going to school with that . . . that hairy savage?'

'Leave it to me,' said Mr Priddle. 'I'm watching their every move. It's all down here.'

He showed her the notes he'd made in his *Troll Watch Diary*.

'As soon as we've got enough evidence we'll call the police.'

Troll at School

ULRIK gazed at himself in the bathroom mirror. He liked his new school uniform. True, the shirt was a bit on the small side. It only reached to his belly button and the trousers looked more like shorts.

Nevertheless, he felt he looked smart. When he went downstairs his mother gave him a big huggle, lifting him right off the ground.

'Is this my little Ulrik?' she said. 'All growned up!'

'Get off, Mum!' protested Ulrik, wiping away the kiss she planted on his cheek.

'Now, don't forget,' Mrs Troll said. 'Be good and do what your teacher tells you.'

'I *know*, Mum,' said Ulrik. 'I've been talking to Warren. He's in the same class as me.'

'That's nice, hairling,' said Mrs Troll. 'I'm glad you're making friends already.'

Later that morning, Ulrik met his class teacher and gave her his best smile. He thought she looked a bit surprised to see him. Her mouth was hanging open as if she was trying to catch passing flies.

The truth was, nobody had warned Mrs Melly that 'the new boy' was a troll. She had never met one before, though of course she had read about them in story books. She knew they were wild, fierce creatures who made a habit of hiding under bridges. This troll was almost as big as her and he was showing his two sharp teeth.

'You must be Ulrik,' she said a little nervously.

'Yes,' said Ulrik. 'And you're Mrs Smelly.'

The class dissolved into fits of giggles.

'Quiet!' barked the teacher. 'My name is Mrs *Melly*, Ulrik, Mrs Melly. Welcome to Class 4.'

She held out her hand to him. Ulrik remembered what Warren had taught him. It seemed a strange way to greet a teacher but then teachers were funny and he didn't want to be rude. He bit Mrs Melly's hand as hard as he could.

'Yargh!' Mrs Melly pulled her hand away and stared at the two sharp fang marks imprinted upon it.

'You bit me!' she said in astonishment.

'Did I do it right?' asked Ulrik.

Mrs Melly had turned a deep shade of purple.

'At this school we do not *bite*,' she said icily.

'Oh. But Warren said . . .'

'You will sit down, Ulrik,' said Mrs Melly. 'And

if you *dare* to bite anyone again, I shall send you straight to the head.'

Ulrik hung his head and slunk away to sit down. He had done exactly what Warren had told him, so why was his teacher so cross? He had so wanted to make a good impression on his first day and get a gold star.

An idea came into his head. When he wanted to please his parents he showed them how his roaring practice was coming on. Warren had assured him Mrs Melly would love to see it. Maybe she wouldn't scowl so much when she saw how hard he'd been practising.

Ulrik took a deep breath. He faced Mrs Melly and tromped down the aisle, stamping his feet in the ant-crushing style his dad had taught him.

'*Graaarr!*' he roared. '*Graarrr!*'

Mrs Melly was certain the troll was going to attack her. It was obviously working itself up into a rage. She backed away until she was up against her desk, then sat down on top of it.

'Now, stop that, Ulrik,' she said.

'GRAAARRR!' roared Ulrik, making the windows rattle.

Mrs Melly overbalanced backwards and disappeared from sight with a yelp.

Looking rather shaken, she emerged from underneath her desk and put her glasses straight. Ulrik looked pleased with himself.

'Uggsome! That was my best roar ever!' he said, beaming. But Mrs Melly didn't seem pleased at all. She sent him to stand outside the head's office.

Mr Wiseman sat him down and talked for a long time. He said that biting, stamping and roaring was shocking behaviour and he hoped Ulrik didn't behave like that at home. Ulrik answered truthfully that he did, but that only seemed to make matters worse. Finally he was sent back to the class.

Mrs Melly sat him next to a girl called Nisha. Nisha moved her chair as far away from him as possible. None of the children sitting at the table spoke a single word to him all day. They all seemed to think he was going to try and bite them. Even Warren pretended not to notice when Ulrik waved at him across the class.

When the bell finally went for the end of school, he was glad he could go home.

'Now,' said Mrs Melly. 'Don't forget – Wednesday is our trip to the farm. Ulrik, here is a letter to take home to your parents. And I shall expect you to be on your best behaviour, is that clear?'

Ulrik nodded miserably. He was beginning to see why trolls didn't go to school.

The Sweet Stink of Home

WHILE Ulrik went to school, Mr Troll got up late as usual. He came downstairs feeling as hungry as a very hungry horse. Since arriving in Biddlesden he'd had very little to eat. Trolls have enormous appetites and would look on an entire roast chicken as little more than a tasty snack. As Mr Troll thumped downstairs he fancied he smelled the delicious aroma of goat coming from the kitchen. But it turned out he had imagined it. When he sat down, Mrs Troll placed a can on the table.

He groaned. 'Oh no, not blunking bean again!'

'No,' said Mrs Troll. 'This is different. It's called spagotty hoops.'

Mr Troll prodded the can glumly. 'Do I have to throw it at the wall?'

Mrs Troll shook her head. 'I asked the lady in the shop. She gave me one of these to open it.' She held up a tin opener with a sharp, hooked blade.

Mr Troll yawned as his wife tried to work out what to do with the tin opener. In the end she raised it high in the air like a dagger, and plunged it into the heart of the can. There was a puncturing THWUCK! Mrs Troll wiped a squirt of tomato sauce from her eye and examined the hole she'd made. 'Hmm,' she said.

BANG! THWUCK! BANG! She attacked the can again and again until it had as many holes as a string vest. 'Pass me your bowl, Eggy,' she said, panting for breath.

Mrs Troll held the can over the bowl and dribbled some stringy globs of spaghetti hoops into it.

'Ugh!' said Mr Troll, peering at the bowl in disgust. 'Looks like maggot soup.'

He pushed back his chair and headed for the door.

'You haven't had any breakfast,' said Mrs Troll.

'I'd rather eat bat droppings,' replied Mr Troll sulkily.

'Oh well, suit yourself,' said Mrs Troll. 'You do the shopping if you're so fussy.'

She followed him into the hall. 'Now where are you going?'

'Out,' growled Mr Troll shortly and slammed the door behind him.

Mr Troll stomped off down Mountain View in the worst of moods. It's well known that trolls can be bad-tempered in the mornings, but a troll who has started the day without breakfast in his belly is the kind of troll it's better to avoid. If there had been a thought bubble above Mr Troll's head it would have been filled with a big black cloud.

As he reached the main road he headed into town without the slightest idea where he was going. Shoppers saw him coming and crossed to the other side of the road to avoid him. Most of them had never seen a fully grown troll before and they certainly didn't expect to meet one stomping along Biddlesden High Street on a grey Monday morning. Cars whizzed past like flies buzzing in his ear. Mr Troll didn't like the noise or the smell they made. He longed to smell the sweet stink of another troll. Back home he might have run into one of his friends, Snorvik or Boglov, and he would have greeted them with a loud roar and a mighty huggle. But here the only creatures to be seen were pasty-faced peeples who flattened themselves against walls to let him go past.

He came to a set of steps leading down into a subway. It looked dark down there. Mr Troll went down the steps hoping to find some kind of cave. The subway was dingy and deliciously smelly. A rumbling sound came from above him as cars passed overhead.

It reminded Mr Troll of the old wooden bridge back home where he used to hide and wait for the skinny goats to pass by. 'Trip-trop, trip-trop,' their little hooves would go on the bridge. How he enjoyed the moment when he sprang up like a jack-in-the-box to give them the fright of their lives. The look of surprise on their silly goat faces!

He closed his eyes, imagining he was back home again under the creaky, old bridge. He could hear footsteps descending the steps into the subway. Mr Troll felt an urge to give something a thumping good fright. A roar was swelling up from deep inside him . . .

Meanwhile, back home, Mrs Troll was waiting for him to return. At first she was cross with him. *Grouchy old grump-bag*, she thought, *storming out like that just because he didn't like his breakfast*. Well, let him go hungry. What did he expect her to do: produce goats out of a hat?

But as the hours passed by she started to become rather anxious. She was used to Mr Troll's sulks, but normally they didn't last longer than an hour or so. Yet when Ulrik returned from school there was still no sign of her husband.

Mrs Troll stood at the window, looking along the road anxiously.

'Hi, Mum,' said Ulrik. 'What are you doing? Where's Dad?'

'That's the trouble,' replied Mrs Troll. 'He went tromping off down the road this morning and I haven't seen him since. Oh Ulrik, I do hope he's all right! He's never been far from the house before. What could have happened?'

Ulrik didn't know. He had wanted to tell his mum about his miserable day at school, but she seemed too worried to listen. He went and stood next to her, resting his head against her shoulder.

Just then a police car pulled up outside the house. A man and a woman in smart black uniforms got out. One of them opened the back door and out climbed Mr Troll.

'Thank uggness!' said Mrs Troll, and hurried to answer the door.

'Is this your husband, madam?' asked the police-woman.

'Eggy? I've been worried sick. Where have you been?' asked Mrs Troll.

'I'm afraid he's been making a bit of a nuisance of himself,' said the policeman. 'We found him in a subway under the high street.'

'Oh Eggy!'

Mr Troll looked down at his feet, embarrassed. 'I just wanted somewhere to hide, somewhere dark and stinksome. I only meant to fright them a bit, that's all.'

The policeman looked at him. 'You did that all right. Scared the living daylights out of them, jumping out and shouting like that.'

'Roaring,' corrected Mr Troll. 'I was roaring. *Grarrr!*'

'Don't start again,' said the policewoman sharply. 'We had enough of that in the car.'

'Are you going to prison, Dad?' asked Ulrik, tugging at his dad's arm.

'Not this time, son,' replied the policeman.

'We'll let him off with a warning. But from now on he'd better behave himself. No more lurking in dark subways. No more scaring folks out of their wits. Nearly gave that old lady a heart attack, you did!'

Mr Troll remembered and smiled. 'Her teeth jumped right out,' he told Ulrik. 'I never did that to a goat!'

'It's not something to be proud of,' said the policewoman sternly.

Mr Troll tried to listen while the police talked for a long time about 'not looking for trouble'. He explained he hadn't been looking for trouble, he had been looking for a cave. But then the conversation got a bit muddled. Finally Mrs Troll saw the police out. When she opened the front door however there was someone else waiting outside: the neighbours from next door. It was turning into a strange day.

Mr Priddle had seen the police car pull up outside the trolls' house through his telescope and had hurried round with his wife.

'Are you arresting them?' he demanded hopefully.

'No, sir,' said the policeman. 'Just a misunderstanding – there's nothing to worry about.'

'That's easy for you to say. You're not living next door to them,' replied Mrs Priddle.

'It's all in here, officer,' said Mr Priddle, brandishing his *Troll Watch Diary*. 'All the evidence you need. Noise at all hours of the morning, biting people . . .'

'Biting?' said Mrs Troll. 'We've never bitten anyone!'

Ulrik hung back behind his mum and said nothing.

'Ask them,' said Mr Priddle, pointing. 'Ask them why there's a dirty great pile of earth in their garden. Ask them what they're eating for dinner tonight!'

Mr and Mrs Troll looked at each other. 'Bean,' said Mr Troll, gloomily. 'It'll be that or maggot soup.'

After much argument the Priddles were eventually persuaded to return to their house.

'Don't worry, we'll keep an eye on them, madam,' said the policeman.

'A fat help that will be when we're all murdered in our beds,' replied Mrs Priddle.

'Why don't we all have a nice cup of tea to calm down?' suggested the policewoman.

'If somebody else mentions tea,' said Mrs Priddle, 'I'm going to scream very loudly.'

Next door the trolls sat round the table, sunk in gloom.

'Well,' said Mrs Troll. 'What was that all about?'

Mr Troll propped his head in his hands. 'It's no good,' he said. 'It's all my fault. We should never have come here.'

'We've only been here a few days,' Mrs Troll pointed out.

'I miss the mountains,' brooded Mr Troll. 'I miss our stinksome old cave. I miss goat pie. I miss hiding under bridges and frighting goatses.'

'It was you who wanted to leave home, Eggy,' Mrs Troll reminded him.

For a while they all sat in dismal silence.

'Ulrik, I completely forgot,' said Mrs Troll, suddenly. 'How was your first day at school?'

'Oh . . . uggsome,' said Ulrik feebly.

'You see, Eggy?' said Mrs Troll. 'Everything's going to work out fine. Ulrik's doing well at school and making lots of new friends, aren't you, hairling?'

'Yes,' lied Ulrik. 'Lots.'

His mum and dad beamed at him fondly. How could he tell them the truth – that his first day at school had been a complete disaster? That he had no friends and no one spoke to him. His parents

had enough to worry about already. Instead he
took out Mrs Melly's letter and gave it to his
mum. Mrs Troll read it through. 'A trip to a farm!'
she said. 'That sounds like fun!'

Goblins!

THAT night Mrs Priddle couldn't sleep. She had been tossing and turning for hours. Every creak and groan of the house made her tremble like a leaf. At last she gave up and shook her husband by the shoulder. Mr Priddle grunted and rolled over.

'Wake up, Roger!' said Mrs Priddle.

'Eh? What's happening?'

'I can't sleep!'

Mr Priddle groaned. 'Whassamatter?' he mumbled.

'I told you, I can't sleep. How can you lie there snoring like a pig when there are murderers living next door? What if I'm next, Roger? What if that brute comes for me in the night and snatches me away.'

At least I would get some sleep, thought Mr Priddle.

'What do you expect me to do, Jackie?' he asked. 'You heard the police. They don't believe us.'

'Then we'll have to *make* them believe. We need proof, Roger. Proof that they . . . I can hardly say the word . . .' She lowered her voice to a whisper. 'Proof that they *eat* children.'

'What sort of proof?' Mr Priddle asked. 'I can't just go next door and start poking around for evidence.'

Mrs Priddle fixed her husband with a steely look he knew all too well.

'No, Jackie,' he said. 'No, I can't . . .'

'You've seen that big pile of earth in their garden. What else is it for?' said Mrs Priddle. 'That's where they *bury* them, Roger. The bones. Think of it – there may be skulls and skeletons and all sorts.' Mr Priddle was thinking and he didn't much like the sound of it.

'There's our proof,' insisted Mrs Priddle. 'If we take a bag of bones to the police they'll *have* to believe us.'

Mr Priddle lay down again. He had to get up for work in a few hours. 'We'll talk about it tomorrow,' he murmured. But his wife's hand gripped his shoulder.

'No, Roger, tonight. I can't put up with another night like this. My nerves won't stand it. You have to go tonight.'

Fifteen minutes later the Priddles held a counsel of war in the kitchen. Warren had heard his parents talking and came downstairs to find out why everyone was up. When he heard about the raid next door, he begged to be allowed to take part. If his dad was going to creep around someone's garden in the dead of night, he wanted to be there – especially if there was the chance of digging up some human bones. Mr Priddle made a show of protesting, but secretly he was glad of the company. The thought of sneaking into the trolls' garden in the dark terrified him.

He was wearing his best black sweater and his face was smeared with dirt. Leaves and twigs stuck out of his floppy gardening hat. He had once seen a film where tough commandos dressed this way so that the enemy wouldn't spot them in the dark (though he didn't remember them wearing gardening hats). Warren's face was masked by the navy balaclava his grandma had knitted him for Christmas. Both of them were armed with torches and spades.

'Right,' said Mr Priddle, trying to sound brave and determined. He glanced at the clock. Four a.m. Soon it would be getting light. He wondered if he would live to see the dawn.

The first problem was climbing over the fence without making a racket. Warren stood on his dad's back and managed to get a foot on the top before jumping over.

'Are you all right, my lambkin?' whispered Mrs Priddle.

'Fine,' came the reply. 'Come on, Dad! Hurry up. It's easy!'

Mr Priddle tried to haul himself up on to the fence, but found his leg wouldn't reach.

'Give me a leg up, Jackie!' he said.

'No thank you. You've got dirty shoes on,' Mrs Priddle replied.

'Come on! Do you want me to go or not?'

'All right, but mind my dressing gown – it's Chinese silk.'

With a lot of pushing and grunting, Mr Priddle managed to get one foot on top of the fence. Gingerly he brought up his other foot. He tried to stand up, tottered for a moment on the top and finally overbalanced, landing on top of something soft.

'OW!' yelped Warren.

'Shhh!' hissed Mr Priddle.

He hoped that trolls slept soundly. What if one of them came out? He would be savaged by a wild, man-eating troll. All they would find of him one day would be a pile of bones and a gardening hat. Mrs Priddle peered at him over the fence.

'Go on, then! Don't just stand there!'

'All right,' he whispered. 'For heaven's sake, Jackie, keep your voice down.'

He shone his torch at the huge pile of earth near the end of the garden. It looked bigger in the dark – like some weird-looking mountain. His hands were trembling. 'Stay calm,' he told himself, 'It's just a pile of earth, that's all. Earth and possibly skeletons. Human skulls. Nothing to be scared of.'

He took several steps towards the mountain. Then the ground disappeared and he fell down into a deep hole with a startled cry. 'Arrrooof!'

Inside the house, Mr Troll was woken by a loud noise. For a moment he thought he was back in his cave in the mountains, but then he felt the soft mattress beneath him – and remembered where he was. Was it the cry of a wolf or a bear that had woken him, or had he imagined it?

Getting up, he looked out of the back window. He caught sight of a tiny beam of light moving in the darkness.

'What is it, hairling?' asked Mrs Troll's sleepy voice.

'Goblins,' said Mr Troll grimly. 'There are goblins outside.'

It was true Mr Troll had never actually met a goblin, but he knew all about them. His grandmother had warned him about goblins when he was a little troggler. Goblins were after your gold. They came in the night with their pointy ears and their sacks over their backs. It made little difference that Mr Troll didn't have any gold – that wouldn't stop goblins. Well, he would give them a nasty surprise. He would teach them a lesson.

He crept into Ulrik's room and shook him, placing a hand over his mouth to stop him crying out.

'Shh! There's goblins in the garden,' he whispered.

Ulrik sat up in bed. 'Goblins? Uggsome! Can I see them?'

'Get dressed sharpish,' said Mr Troll. This is a chance for you to do some proper roaring. I want you to roar so loud you fright the bogles out of them.'

Outside in the garden, Mr Priddle had managed to clamber out of the hole with the help of Warren. Now they made their way to the foot of the earth mountain.

'Where do we dig?' asked Warren.

'I don't know. Anywhere,' said Mr Priddle. 'As soon as we find anything, let's get back over that fence.'

'You're not scared, are you, Dad?' asked Warren. 'Your hands are shaking.'

'Don't be ridiculous, Warren,' snapped Mr Priddle. He dug his spade into the earth but then froze with terror. Out of the dark, a blood-curdling roar reached his ears.

'GRRAAAARR!'

It was followed by a second, not-quite-as-blood-curdling roar from Ulrik.

'*Graaarr!*'

Mr Priddle shone his torch up the garden. Two angry trolls had burst from the house and were thundering towards them across the lawn. He could see their massive black shapes and their sharp white fangs. Beneath his feet the ground was shaking like an earthquake.

'Dad! What do we do?' yelped Warren.

'Run!' said Mr Priddle, and to show what he meant he dropped his spade and streaked towards the fence faster than a greyhound.

If it hadn't been for the dark, things might have gone badly for the Priddles. An angry troll defending his cave can be ferocious. He will tromp on his enemy with both feet. He will pick them up by the ears and bounce them around like a rubber ball. But this didn't happen to the Priddles because they switched off their torches and no one could see a blind thing in the dark.

Ulrik roared and Mr Troll roared.

Warren cried: 'Dad! Don't leave me!'

Mr Priddle remembered that in his panic he'd left his son behind just before he fell into the gigantic muddy hole for a second time.

Meanwhile, at the foot of the earth hill, Mr Troll caught hold of someone who gave him a hard kick in the shins.

'Yah! Ulrik, that's me,' he said.

'Sorry Dad, I thought you were a goblins.'

'Over there – they're getting away,' pointed Mr Troll, seeing two shadows running for the fence.

Mr Priddle had managed to climb out of the

hole and was now clambering over the fence with surprising agility. Warren wasn't so lucky – he wasn't tall enough to pull himself up.

On the other side of the fence, Mr Priddle found his wife waiting for him anxiously.

'Where's Warren?' she asked.

'Run!' gasped her husband.

'But where's my lambkin?'

'Mum! Help!' came Warren's terrified voice from the other side of the fence.

Mr Priddle reached over. 'Grab my hand!' he ordered.

But as Warren was hauled up by his dad, he felt another pair of hands grab him by the legs.

'I've got one, Dad!' cried Ulrik.

'Where are you?' said Mr Troll, who had blundered into a wheelbarrow.

'Over here, Dad!'

Mr Priddle pulled and Ulrik pulled. Warren was the rope in a game of tug of war. But something was starting to slip down his legs and he decided it was no time for preserving his dignity.

Ulrik fell back on the grass, clutching a pair of trousers.

There was a thump from the other side of the fence and footsteps hurried away.

'What happened?' said Mr Troll, arriving at last.

Ulrik showed him the pair of black school trousers. 'He left these behind,' he said.

Mr Troll held up the muddy trousers and examined them. 'Whew!' he said. 'Biggest goblins I ever heard of.'

How to Make Friends

U LRIK woke up. The first thing he remembered was that he had to go to school. School today, school tomorrow and the day after. Yesterday morning he had been so eager to find out what school was like, but now he wished he could just stay at home. He liked his new bedroom. It was cosier now it had a thick layer of mud and leaves on the floor. His mum had promised to look for some cow-patties to make it nice and stinksome. He'd begun a mud-painting on the wall over his bed – a picture of him playing 'Roar and Sneak' with his friends in the forest.

The worst thing about school, Ulrik thought, were the 'playtimes', which happened twice a day. Peeples seemed to play differently from trolls and he wasn't sure how to join in.

His mum stuck her head round the door. 'Ulrik, time to get up!'

'Uhhh!' groaned Ulrik. 'I don't feel very well.'

'Don't you, my ugglesome? What's the matter?'

'I think I've got the bellies-ache.'

'Oh dear, you poor little troggler,' said his mum. 'Let me see.'

Ulrik pulled up his nightshirt to show his round belly. His mum gave him a playful poke in the ribs.

'Ha ha hee! Don't do that!' he giggled, rolling around.

'You don't seem too bad to me. Hurry up and get dressed – breakfast's ready,' said Mrs Troll.

Ulrik plodded downstairs in his school uniform. His dad was already at the breakfast table. Ulrik noticed he had baked bean juice smeared round his mouth.

'I thought you didn't like it,' he said.

'I was hungry,' said Mr Troll. 'That was fun last night, eh? You and me chasing goblins.'

'Yes,' said Ulrik. 'Did I do OK?'

'You were uggsome,' said his dad. 'The roaring still needs work, but it's coming on.'

'I've been practising,' said Ulrik. 'You were scary, Dad!'

'I was, wasn't I?' beamed Mr Troll. 'Frighted the

bogles out of them. Those goblins won't be coming back to rob us again.'

'My hairy, scary old husband,' laughed Mrs Troll, kissing him on the snout.

Ulrik smiled. He was glad to see his parents looking happy again. Chasing robbers round the garden in the dead of night was just what his dad needed to cheer him up.

Ulrik still had the muddy trousers their visitor had left behind, though personally he wasn't convinced they belonged to a goblin. Inside the label of the trousers he had found the letters 'WP' scrawled in red letters. Ulrik had thought it over and WP didn't sound like the name of a goblin. It sounded more like Warren Priddle. He hadn't told his parents his suspicions. There was always the chance his dad would throw a tantrum and storm next door.

Ulrik ate his baked bean slowly, drinking it cold through the holes in the tin. Soon it would be time for school and he wanted to put off the moment as long as possible.

'Dad,' he said, 'you've got lots of friends, haven't you?'

'Lots back home,' agreed Mr Troll.

'But where did you get them?' asked Ulrik.

Mr Troll looked puzzled. It seemed a funny question. 'I didn't really *get* them,' he said. 'Snorvik and Boglov have been my friends since I was a little troggler.'

'But you must have started somewhere. I mean, what do you *do* when you want to be friends?'

'Do?' Mr Troll glanced worriedly at Mrs Troll. He'd never really thought about it. He cleared his throat. 'Well,' he said. 'Say I run into Snorvik, right?'

'Yes,' said Ulrik, paying close attention.

'First off, I'd give him a great big huggle. Lift him clean off the ground. Then he'd roar and I'd roar back and he'd roar again, and we'd argue about who roars the loudest. Then we'd go off and look for some goatses to chase.'

Mr Troll sat back in his chair, looking pleased with himself. It seemed to him this perfectly summed up the nature of friendship. But it didn't seem to satisfy Ulrik.

'Oh,' he said in a disappointed voice, and got down from the table. 'Thanks for breakfast, Mum.'

'What the bogles was that about then?' asked Mr Troll, mystified.

'I don't know,' said Mrs Troll. 'He does seem a bit quiet.'

Later Ulrik trudged along the road on his way to school. *Maybe today will be better*, he thought. He would be careful not to bite Mrs Melly and not to roar in class. If he was quiet, and tried not to look too big, perhaps the other children wouldn't stare at him as if he was about to gobble them up.

Morning lessons passed without any trouble. When the bell went for break, Ulrik trooped outside with the others. He leaned against the railings, trying to look harmless and friendly. The shrieks and laughter from all corners of the playground only made him feel more alone. Everyone else seemed to have friends to play with. His classmates were playing football, swapping cards, skipping over ropes and talking in groups, but no one came near him. He wondered if he should run up to one of them and give them a mighty huggle. That's what his dad would have done. But they might scream and think he was trying to hurt them.

One of the teachers, Miss Leach, was patrolling the playground followed by a gaggle of small children.

Some boys ran past him, chasing each other. Ulrik recognised Warren and called out to him. Warren stopped.

'Oh. What do you want?' he said.

'Have you lost your trousers?' Ulrik enquired.

Warren looked uncomfortable. 'What? Are you being funny?'

'No,' said Ulrik. 'It's just – weren't you in our garden last night?'

'Don't be stupid. I was in bed!' snorted Warren, turning a deeper shade of red.

'Oh,' said Ulrik. Perhaps he'd made a mistake.

The other boys had gathered round him, hands on hips. 'What are you playing?' Ulrik asked. 'Can I play?'

Danny pointed at Ulrik. 'We're not playing with him. He's too ugly.'

'And he bites,' added Rashid.

'I won't,' promised Ulrik. He sucked in his fangs so that he looked toothless.

'Come on, why don't we let him play?' said Warren unexpectedly.

'Can I?'

'Yeah,' said Warren. 'It'll be fun.' He turned to his friends and gave them a sly wink.

'You can be "On", Ulrik,' he said.

Ulrik beamed. 'Uggsome! On what?'

'Duh!' said Warren. 'It means you've got to chase us.'

'And catch us,' added Rashid.

'All right. Then what?' asked Ulrik.

'Nothing. Whoever you catch is "On". That's the game.'

'Oh, OK.' It seemed too easy. At home Ulrik and his friends played 'Pongo' – a game similar to

'Chase' only smellier. But Ulrik didn't explain the rules of 'Pongo'*, he did as he was told and counted to ten while Warren and his friends ran off.

'Eight . . . nine . . . ten!' he shouted and hurried after them.

Although he was much bigger, the boys were quicker on their feet and dodged him time and again. 'Yah! Missed me!' they taunted.

Ulrik kept chasing them doggedly, till at last he cornered Warren, who was hiding behind rows of plants. 'Ul-rik!' sang Warren. 'Come and get me!'

Ulrik didn't really see the garden in its neat stone border. He just trampled straight across it. Tomatoes, lettuces and sweet peas were squashed to a pulp beneath his size ten feet.

'Ulrik! GET OFF THERE!' a voice boomed across the playground.

---

* *In 'Pongo' the catcher is blindfolded and has to find the other trolls purely by using his sense of smell. If he catches one he sits on them and shouts 'Pongo, Pongo, you are ongo!' If he walks into a tree and knocks himself out, he loses.*

Ulrik turned to see Miss Leach pointing an angry finger at him.

'Oh Ulrik!' said Warren. 'Trampling on the school garden. Now you're really for it!'

Danny and Rashid smirked as Ulrik was led away by Miss Leach. Once again he found himself sitting outside the head's office. Once again he had to endure a long, serious lecture. Mr Wiseman said it had taken months to grow the vegetables in the school garden, but it had only taken him a few seconds to destroy them.

'I'm afraid you must be taught a lesson, Ulrik,' he said. 'No trip to the farm tomorrow; instead you will stay behind and work.'

Ulrik nodded sadly. He'd been looking forward to the trip to the farm. But now he wasn't allowed to go. So far the only thing he'd learned at school was how to get into trouble.

Bubble Trouble

BACK home, Mrs Troll was dirtying the house. She had noticed a number of ugly clean patches in the dining room. It took a lot of effort dragging in mud and leaves from outside. The house lacked the homely stench of their old cave. Mr Troll had grumbled about it that very morning. 'If you think it's so stinkless, bring home some cow-patties,' she'd told him. So he had gone out to look for a cow-patty shop and now she was all alone.

Once she had dirtied the house, she sat down at

the table. There wasn't a great deal to do. At home she would have taken a walk down to The Hubblings – the natural pools at the foot of Troll Mountain where warm water bubbled up from under the ground. Mrs Troll would sit for hours in the bubbling soup with her friends, listening to them grumble about their husbands or the sunny weather. Sometimes they made bubbles of their own.*

Mrs Troll missed chatting to her friends at The Hubblings. She had tried sitting in the bath upstairs but it was no fun talking to yourself. *Perhaps I should get out of the house and visit someone*, she thought. *But who?* She didn't know anyone in Biddlesden. Once or twice she'd seen the peeples next door staring at her over the fence or from an upstairs window. The skinny bald one was called Roger and she'd heard him call his mate 'Darling'. So far Darling and Roger didn't seem very friendly, but Mrs Troll was prepared to

---

*   *Trolls call this 'a gruffler'. It is a troll custom to let loose a gruffler after a meal to show your appreciation.*

make allowances. *Peeples are shy*, she thought. *Not like trolls*. Why not go next door and take Darling a present to show that she wanted to be friends?

She looked round the room for a suitable gift and her eye fell on the small pile of rocks on the table. Trolls collect rocks the way some people collect fridge magnets or china cats. In particular they are fond of rocks which bear any resemblance to a troll. In the garden Mrs Troll had found a rock that reminded her of a troll's bottom, which she was very proud of. She was sure Darling would like it.

Clutching her present, she went next door.

Number 8, Mountain View appeared to be empty, but music was coming from somewhere inside. After knocking on the door several times, Mrs Troll walked round the side of the house and peered through the windows. There was no one in the kitchen or in the small room next to it. But at the next window she could hear the music plainly and pushed her nose up against the glass.

Inside, Mrs Priddle was taking a bath. After the frightening events of the night before she had got up late and filled the bath tub to the top with bubbles. From the lounge she was listening to her favourite 'pan-pipes' CD, which she found relaxing in times of stress. If she shut her eyes she could pretend that everything was normal. There were no dangerous trolls living next door, no bones buried in the garden and nothing to make her nervous. She sank lower in the bath, so that the bubbles rose up to her chin.

Outside, Mrs Troll was trying hard to catch her attention through the window. She waved the rock in her hand to show that she'd brought a present, but the rippled glass made it hard to see, especially as it was misted up on the inside. She rapped loudly on the window.

Mrs Priddle's eyes blinked open and she caught sight of the monstrous shadow of the troll at the window. Its huge ugly face pressed against the glass, the snout squished to one side. It was smiling horribly. Mrs Priddle gave a shrill scream and sank down out of sight. 'Roblobb!' she gurgled, which is how the name 'Roger' sounds when you say it underwater. But her husband had gone to work and would not be back until six. Warren was at school. She was all alone in the house and not wearing a stitch. Surely this was some horrible nightmare?

The troll had a weapon in its hand – a rock that it was shaking at her. Maybe it was going to smash the window! Mrs Troll thought of trying to reach the phone in the lounge, but that meant getting out of the bath and she was too rigid with fear to move. If she just stayed where she was, perhaps her unwanted visitor would give up and go away.

The troll was tapping on the window, making muffled sounds which might have been threats. At last its dark shadow vanished. Mrs Priddle held her breath, listening to the heavy tread of footsteps on the gravel path outside. A moment later she heard it again at the back of the house, rattling the door. It was trying to get in! She remembered something that made her blood run cold. Sometimes Roger went out in the morning and left the back door unlocked. She had told him about it a thousand times. What if today was one of those days? Mrs Priddle looked around desperately for some kind of weapon. The only thing she could find was Warren's plastic water pistol lying next to the soap dish.

There was the click of a door opening, followed by a loud slam. The troll was in the house! Mrs Priddle lay under her white blanket of bubbles, not daring to move.

'Hello, Darling!' called a voice. 'It's me!'

Mrs Priddle didn't answer. The troll was trying to trick her into thinking it was her husband. But she wasn't that stupid. Roger didn't have a deep, growly voice and his footsteps didn't sound like a giant doing a war dance.

She could hear the troll moving through the downstairs rooms, searching for her. For a few seconds everything went quiet and she dared to hope it had gone away. Then a large hairy head popped round the door.

'Ah! There you are!' smiled Mrs Troll.

Mrs Priddle stared at her. She pointed the water pistol with two trembling hands.

'Don't come any closer or I'll fire,' she said.

Mrs Troll held out the odd-shaped rock in her hand.

'I brought you this, Darling,' she said. 'It looks like a bottom. Not your bottom of course but still, you could put it somewhere. Where do you want it?'

Mrs Troll was doing her best to be chatty, but her neighbour didn't respond, she just kept pointing the thing in her hand. Perhaps it was a gift and she wanted to make a swap? It was hard to tell. Mrs Troll reached out for the water pistol and a jet of water squirted her in the eye.

'Oooh!' said Mrs Troll. It had made a wet patch down the front of her dress.

'Please . . .' whimpered Mrs Priddle. 'Please!'

'What is it, Darling?' asked Mrs Troll. It was clear to her Mrs Priddle wanted something, but she seemed too shy to ask. Steam rose from the bath water and the bubbles looked inviting. Mrs Troll thought of The Hubblings and how she used to sit and chat with her friends. Perhaps Darling was inviting her to get in?

'Room for a little one?' she said. 'You'll have to move over.'

Mrs Priddle didn't realise what was happening until the troll unzipped her dress and started to get into the bath. Then she shot out of the bath like a cork from a bottle.

Pausing only to grab a towel, she ran down the hall and right out of the front door. Her screams could be heard four streets away.

'HELP! Murder! Somebody save me!'

Left alone, Mrs Troll wiped some bubbles from

her snout. She climbed out of the bath with a weary sigh and got dressed. She left the bottom-shaped rock on the television before closing the front door quietly. 'Peeples are very strange,' she said to herself.

That night, in bed, she told Egbert the whole puzzling story.

'And then the polices came back,' she concluded. '"More complaints,"' they said. '"Breaking into peeples' houses. Frighting the neighbours."'

'Frighting them?' snorted Mr Troll. 'You only took her a rock to be friendly, for uggness' sake.'

'I know,' said Mrs Troll. 'Serves me right for trying to be nice.'

'They're as mad as bees in a bottle,' said Mr Troll. 'I asked for some fresh cow-patties in a shop this morning and they looked at me as if I was talking hogswoggle.'

'I know,' said Mrs Troll. 'I don't think we'll ever get used to it. We've got no friends, the house doesn't smell right, and every day the polices call round.'

'Huh!' grunted Mr Troll. 'At least Ulrik has got friends.'

'I hope so,' said Mrs Troll doubtfully. 'He doesn't talk about school much. He's got this farm trip tomorrow, but he hasn't said a word about it.' She rested her head on Mr Troll's shoulder. 'Eggy?'

'Mmm?'

'Couldn't we just go home?'

'No,' said Mr Troll gruffly. 'I told you.'

'I'm sure the goat thing has blown over. No one wants to make fun of you.'

'Oh no,' said Mr Troll, with heavy sarcasm. 'I'm

sure they'll never mention it.' He imitated Snorvik's booming voice. 'Look, here comes old Egbert. Run into any monster goatses lately, Eggy? Fallen off any bridges?'

Mrs Troll patted his round belly. 'It could have happened to anyone, hairling.'

'I can't go back,' said Mr Troll stubbornly. 'We've got to make the best of it here.'

Mrs Troll sighed. Mr Troll sighed. He got out of bed and tromped up and down it a few times, to see if it made him feel better. It didn't 'Come on,' he said at last.

'Where are we going?' asked Mrs Troll. 'It's the middle of the night!'

'Somewhere more comfortable. We'll wake Ulrik.'

Twenty minutes later they were all huddled in the cold, damp subway under the high street.

'It's stinksome,' said Ulrik, sniffing the air.

'It is, isn't it?' said Mr Troll. 'Close your eyes and you can imagine you're back in our own buggly old cave.'

Ulrik closed his eyes and tried to imagine being home. He imagined the drip drip of water and the sweet, earthy stench of their cave, the wind moaning outside like an ogre with toothache.

Above them the city streets were empty and only the occasional rumble told of a car passing overhead.

Ulrik snuggled between his mum and dad for warmth. Soon it would be daylight and that meant school. He hadn't told his parents that he was banned from going on the school trip. Neither had he mentioned that he'd bitten his teacher or trampled on the school garden. Sooner or later they were bound to find out though, and that was the worst part of all.

Big Bad Goat

'HE can't stay there on his own,' said Mrs Melly. She glanced through the classroom window, where Ulrik was sitting all by himself.

'I told him he was to stay behind,' said Mr Wiseman. 'I made it quite clear.'

'I know,' said Mrs Melly, 'but nobody will have him. I've asked every teacher in the school and none of them wants a troll sitting at the back of their class all day. They say he upsets the other children.'

'Then what are we going to do?' asked the head.

'Can't he stay with you?' asked Mrs Melly.

'Be serious! I can't have him in my office – I've got parents coming to see me. What if he bites somebody?'

Mrs Melly sighed. 'Then he'll just have to come on the trip after all. Goodness knows I must be out of my mind. Ulrik on a farm – who knows what he'll get up to!'

Ulrik wasn't sure why he was allowed on the trip after all, but he was pleased to be going. On the coach he sat by himself next to the window, while everyone else sat with their friends. Warren was on the back seat with Danny and Rashid. Ulrik could hear them swapping crisps and chocolate bars from their lunch boxes. He wished he was sitting with them and had his own lunch box. He began to hum a tromping song to cheer himself up, but he must have hummed too loudly because across the aisle Nisha and Katy Sims were staring at him and sniggering.

The farmer peeples who showed them round was called Mrs Douglas. Ulrik liked her from the start. She showed them the young lambs in their white, woolly coats and the cows being milked in the barn. She let them feed the pigs and climb over the big red tractor in the corner of the yard. Ulrik asked if he could take a cow-patty home but Mrs Douglas just laughed, as if he had told a very good joke. All the same he was starting to enjoy himself. Beside the yard he spotted an animal with a black, shaggy coat and two long, curly horns. It was all by itself in a pen.

'A goat!' he said.

'Yes, Ulrik,' said Mrs Douglas. 'That's Victor. He's a mountain goat.'

'Can we go in and see him?' asked Mrs Melly.

'No, I'm afraid we keep Victor away from visitors,' replied Mrs Douglas. 'He's got a nasty temper. Get too close and he might butt you.'

Ulrik took a good long look at Victor. He didn't look friendly. Ulrik remembered the giant goat which had tossed his father off the bridge: hooves like iron and horns sharp as knives. Victor looked like that kind of goat.

Later, Mrs Douglas left them in the farmyard to eat their lunch, seated on some bales of hay. On the far side of the yard, Warren leaned over the fence, watching Victor chew the grass. Suddenly there was a scream of alarm from Katy Sims. The gate of the pen had swung open and Victor had trotted out into the farmyard. Warren was standing by the gate with a mischievous smirk on his face. Victor eyed the children in the yard and gave a low, menacing bleat. 'Bahhhh!'

He lowered his horned head and ran at them. Class 4 scattered in all directions, leaving their half-eaten sandwiches behind them. Some ran into the gift shop, while others dived into the barn and bolted the door behind them. Ulrik climbed on top of the red tractor, where he found Mrs Melly looking pale and shaken.

'Mrs Douglas! The goat's got out!' she called.

But there was no answer – Mrs Douglas was too far away to hear them. Victor trotted around the yard in search of a target. Turning his head, he caught sight of the boy who had opened the gate to set him free. The smirk vanished from Warren's face and the colour drained away.

'Warren! Get away from there!' warned Mrs Melly.

But Warren couldn't move. He was rooted to the spot with fear. The goat was staring at him with its small, mean eyes. It snorted.

'Help!' croaked Warren in a small, frightened voice.

There was no time to think. Ulrik jumped down from the tractor. He tromped towards the goat, stamping his feet hard to get Victor's attention. When that didn't work, he took a deep breath and bellowed his best roar: '*GRARRR!*'

It was enough to scatter the sparrows from the trees, but it didn't scare Victor. The goat simply turned its head to see who was making all the noise. It had a black beard wagging from its chin and it looked in an evil mood.

Ulrik tried a second roar but this time it came out as a squeak, like air escaping from a balloon. Faced with a choice of two victims, Victor chose the smaller one and turned his attention back to Warren.

'Stay there, Warren,' called Ulrik. 'I'm coming.'

Ulrik began to inch his way round the yard, keeping close to the fence, until he reached the place where Warren was cornered by the gate.

'Get behind me,' Ulrik whispered.

'What are you going to do?' asked Warren.

Ulrik didn't answer. The truth was he didn't know. His plan had been to distract Victor long enough for Warren to escape from the yard, but now the two of them were trapped together. He bravely stepped in front of Warren, blocking Victor's path. The goat tossed its head impatiently, tired of playing games. It kicked up a cloud of dust and lowered its wicked-looking horns. Ulrik knew it was preparing to charge.

'Run, Ulrik!' called Mrs Melly, peering down from the top of the tractor.

'Run, Ulrik, run!' echoed the voices of Class 4. But Ulrik refused to run. He was a troll and trolls didn't run from goats. His dad hadn't run when he'd faced the giant goat on the bridge. As Victor gathered speed, pounding across the yard towards him, Ulrik did the only thing he could think of. He closed his eyes, opened his mouth and began to sing.

He sang a song of his homeland, of the blue mountains and the shining lakes.

A few paces short of his target, Victor skidded to

an abrupt halt. He put his head on one side to listen. He was a mountain goat and this song brought back a long-forgotten memory of the craggy mountains where he grew up. It filled him with such sadness and longing that a tear ran down his long nose and plopped into the dust.

Ulrik opened his eyes, surprised to find he wasn't flying through the air. When he went closer and stroked Victor's shaggy head, the goat licked his hand and meekly allowed himself to be led back into his pen.

As soon as the gate clicked shut, a great cheer erupted from all around the yard. Ulrik found himself surrounded by his class mates, all talking at once and gazing at him with wide-eyed admiration.

'Ulrik!' said Mrs Melly, giving him a hug. 'That was *so* brave!'

'You were, like, cool!' said Danny.

'You were a hero!' said Nisha dramatically.

Ulrik was glad that no one could see him blushing beneath his hair.

'Now,' said Mrs Melly. 'Where is Warren Priddle?'

Warren came forward, looking very small and shame-faced.

'Warren. Did you open that gate? The truth, please.'

'Yes, Mrs Melly,' mumbled Warren.

'That was a very, very stupid thing to do. If it wasn't for Ulrik here, someone might have got badly hurt. What do you say to him?'

'Thanks, Ulrik,' said Warren sheepishly. He held out his hand. Ulrik opened his mouth to bite it – but just in time, remembered what had happened last time. Instead he did what trolls do to show they are friends. He lifted Warren right off the ground in a mighty troll huggle.

All Together Now

NINE weeks later, at the end of summer term, there was a concert. The parents sat in rows and listened dewy-eyed to their children singing. Sitting in the front row, taking up four seats between them, were Mr and Mrs Troll. They had dressed in their smartest clothes for the occasion. Mr Troll sported a red bow tie to match his Bermuda shorts while Mrs Troll glittered in a yellow ball gown that she was unfortunately wearing back to front. When Ulrik came forward to sing his solo, Mr Troll couldn't help cheering and stamping his large, hairy feet.

Everyone agreed that Ulrik's singing was the highlight of the concert. In fact, Mr and Mrs Troll wept so loudly that they had to be shushed several times. When Ulrik sang, declared Mr Troll afterwards, he could almost smell the pine forests back home.

Afterwards Mr Troll caught sight of the Priddles and invited them back for supper, in a burst of generosity. Since the incident with 'the mad goat' the Priddles had softened a little towards their neighbours. Mrs Priddle no longer screamed when she met one of the trolls on the street. Mr Priddle no longer spied constantly on his neighbours through his telescope. Even Warren admitted that Ulrik wasn't so bad really – for a troll.

Yet, despite their change of heart, none of them had ever actually set foot inside the trolls' house and they were a little nervous about what they would find.

'Phwar! It pongs!' said Warren as soon they came through the front door.

'Warren!' scolded his mum, but Mrs Troll seemed flattered.

'I do my best,' she said. 'I'm afraid the cow-patties aren't as fresh as they were.'

The Priddles picked their way carefully through the mud and leaves on the floor, worried what they might step in. Luckily, since it was a warm day, Mr Troll announced they would all sit outside.

An hour later, things seemed to be going fairly well. They had all politely refused second helpings of Mrs Troll's baked bean and banana pie and were wondering what to talk about next.

Ulrik, who had been waiting for the right moment, appeared from the house with a muddy pair of trousers and dropped them in Warren's lap.

Warren recognised them at once and turned pink. 'Wh . . . whose are these?' he stammered. 'They're not mine!'

'You haven't even looked at them,' said Ulrik.

'Give them to me,' said Mrs Priddle, snatching the trousers impatiently. 'Of course they're yours, Warren! I recognise them. I'd been wondering where these had got to.'

'Mum!' Warren shook his head. 'I've never seen them before!'

'Don't be so silly. Here are your initials on the label – WP. I wrote it myself. Wherever did you find them, Ulrik?'

'Well . . .' began Ulrik, but Mr Troll interrupted him.

'By the bogles!' he said. 'It wasn't goblins in our garden that night, it was you. You were creeping around trying to rob us!'

The Priddles couldn't deny they had been creeping around – the evidence of Warren's trousers proved it. They looked at the ground, ashamed and embarrassed. Mr Priddle took a gulp of Mr Troll's home-made slug-and-nettle wine, forgetting what was in it. When he'd finished choking he tried to explain.

'We didn't want to rob you, Egbert,' he said. 'We were just . . .'

'. . . just looking,' supplied Mrs Priddle.

'In the muddle of the night?' asked Mr Troll. 'Looking for what exactly?'

Mr Priddle gulped. 'Well, for bones actually,' he said. 'You see, Jackie somehow got the idea . . . well, that . . . that trolls eat . . .'

'Eat what?' said Mrs Troll.

'I heard you in the supermarket that day,' said Mrs Priddle. 'You asked for a nice young kid!'

'What's wrong with that?' replied Mrs Troll. 'Goat is Egbert's favourite and a young kid is nice and tendersome.'

The Priddles looked at each other, as their mistake finally dawned on them.

'You mean you were talking about a *goat*?' said Mrs Priddle. 'We thought . . .'

'What?' said Mr Troll. 'That we eat porky little peeples like your Warren?'

The Priddles nodded sheepishly and waited for their neighbours to fly into a rage.

Mr Troll looked at Mrs Troll, then at Ulrik. He puffed out his cheeks and exploded with laughter. All three trolls laughed and held their bellies and kicked their legs in the air.

When they had at last recovered, Mr Priddle said, 'I still don't understand. Why dig up all that earth if it wasn't to bury something?' He pointed at Mr Troll's gigantic earth-hill, now almost as tall as the house.

Mr Troll smiled. 'What's the name of this road?' he asked.

'Mountain View,' replied Mr Priddle.

'Makes no sense,' said Mr Troll. 'There's no mountainses. And no view. Not till now. Come and take a look.'

A minute later the Trolls and the Priddles were all standing on top of Mr Troll's earth-hill. Ulrik often climbed up here when he was feeling a little homesick. He could see right across the houses and gardens to a wood in the distance. It was only a molehill compared to Troll Mountain, but it was their own.

'And now,' announced Mr Troll, 'we are all going to roar.'

'Oh no, please!' protested Mrs Priddle.

'Go on, try it,' urged Mr Troll.

'It makes you feel good!' said Ulrik.

'Deep breath,' instructed Mr Troll. 'Puff out your chests and roar.'

'*GRARRRRR!*'

An ear-splitting roar echoed along Mountain View and over the neatly cut lawns, so that neighbours looked up and wondered if a jet plane was passing over.

Ulrik smiled to himself. Peeples weren't so bad

once you got to know them, he decided. With a bit more hair you would hardly notice how ugly they were.